A Tale of Wilful Non-Compliance

Greig Thomson

DISARTICULATED PRESS

Adelaide

Foreword

Welcome to the narrative delirium! *Disarticulated,* the first book published by *Disarticulated Press,* is an adventure in both the mind and the body.

Disarticulated is a piece of sound art, as much as a

written text. Follow the links at the start of the story, put in your headphones and let T.'s mind enter yours. He will speak directly to you, with music and sound as an audio guide. T.s inner voice is brought to life through the magical narration of my good friend and voice performer, Edward Ingram, adding a depth to the text beyond the words on the page.

***

The voices came thick and fast when I found my rhythm, my unique style, and *Disarticulated* was a reckoning; a moment where the truth spilt out over the page, mixed in with all the exaggeration and delusion. It is a story of the mind (a separate and malevolent entity) speaking directly to the body, T. (the weary traveller), going down the road together, but never getting anywhere fast. Together, they quietly rail against society, the 'factory family', 'bully boys', 'the boar', mental hospitals and disinterested doctors.

As the mind takes over, the story takes a series of handbrake turns, and T. is thrown around the cab, bashed bloody by the weight of mental inertia. Hieronymus Bosch's *Ship of Fools* comes to life, wrecking both mind and body on the shore of a broken reality. I must admit, it was in Foucault's *Madness and Civilisation* that I came across the *Ship of Fools*; one of history's great symbolic societal failures, transporting the mentally unwell to anywhere else, away from the city walls.

And then… spaceships and alien trephinations. The detachment felt during electro-shock therapy is brought to life in a spacecraft medical bay, millions of miles from Earth. There are great snakes slithering along an alligator highway, trolls living under bridges, and a butcher with a boar's head cutting meat in an underwater aquarium. It is all written in the language of psychosis, poured out in front of you so there's nothing to do but manically mop up the subtext pooling all over the floor. In the end, the real symbol that ties it all together is the dandelion. It takes a beating from

the security guards and is ravaged by the seasons, but the
dandelion can't be killed, not that easily.

Now, the adventure awaits. Activate the QR code, put in
your headphones, and follow T.'s inner voice on the journey
through both literal and figurative worlds, back to the
hospital window with a cup of tepid orange juice.

-   Greig Thomson

-   Adelaide, July 7, 2025

This is a multimedia text with voice narration and a digital score. Please access the sound file at either of the following links, and listen as you read:

https://disarticulatedpress.com/published-books/

Dandelions

Can you hear it, T.? The slow rising of the strings, the quiet staccato of the woodwinds. In each harmonic shift, we hear the ups and downs, the modulation in dynamics revealing something inside of us, a latent trembling wave of mania and melancholia. We could always hear music, T. A soundtrack to our lives. Mother called it our "musical ear". It was beyond a compulsion, a gift unique to us. She would smile gently and play with our earlobe, the understated sadness of a parent's understanding that there was more to it, some cerebral abnormality. But there is so much joy within the music, trapped behind the notes in the stave. It seems fitting to remember it now in our captivity. The freedom of expression locked inside the tight western tonality, the cage of notes and arpeggios. The mind is still free, T. We are fluttering like the manic scales, racing through the breakneck intervals, always with an eye for shape and form. Always influenced by changes in expression, the pitches and valleys forming new landscapes in our mind…

***

But let us start at the beginning, with the dandelions, crushed down, trodden by security guards at the end of the garden. The limits of the facility. Time is not an issue here. The dandelions sprout in the warmer weather, beautiful petals, vivid yellow. The rain pads them down but brings them to new life. In the winter, the snow drifts over them, dusting them white, before covering them completely. Suffocating them. Until spring arrives to bring them back from the point of annihilation. And you see it, T., each season. The plight of the dandelions. You see it from the facility window, your wheelchair pushed up to the glass, a side table with tepid orange juice next to you. Your head lolls to one side, your mouth agape. I think your batteries have run out. But the mind, it still runs unimpeded.

I am working in the background, searching through our memories, creating new story arcs, new melodies for future operatic adventures. I am the composer, the conductor, but you'll have to forgive me. I'm prone to exaggeration, sometimes drifting off into sentimentality, abstraction. You and me, T., we're part of the same organism, the mind and the body. The real and the imagined. Nevertheless, without you, I would not be alive at all. So, I want you to listen but listen intently. Listen to the shape of the words, the cadence of ups and downs, the frenzied rhythms of psychosis, the lilting, dolente movements that spiral slowly downward into a well of grief, and all that is in between, the mixed states of melancholy, excitement and joy. Listen, T. Our world was born into the noise around us. Our true life began when you first heard the sound of my voice.

***

The Boar

Wake up and fry the bacon! That dense cooked meat smell, elemental, a hint of dirt from unwashed hands. We wouldn't be carnivores without it. Pig smoke fills our apartment and the sounds of the street below tick-tick like a static toccata, the driving staccato notes of the pedestrians and the hum of the traffic. The passersby can hear us up here, first level, overlooking the street. We get our meat from the butcher below, where the bacon smoke spirals down and plays on the shop front. It travels east too, to the neighbour's window, mixes in with the weed that she smokes passing the joint to Foucault? Jung? David Hasselhoff reaches through the tv and takes a hit, grinning and dropping ash on the rug. The open window bulges under the weight of the street and the sky and the bodies in the buildings are full of repressed minds bursting seams of blood around the membrane of polite society. Our extractor fan farts and rattles, vacuuming up the smoke back through the window, and the machinations of street life are returned to their default settings. There is an old lady outside on the pavement with a tritone shopping bag and a Morrispatterned kerchief. She is disappointed the smoke is gone. No tragedy to meddle in. No story to retell to the care home residents, with herself as the socially conscious bystander. *"And the pity of it all. It's just so sad."* The toast pops and we fumble with it. Butter first, then the bacon. And we put our shirt on as we keep the bacon sandwich in our mouth, a dog eating in gulps and spluttered chews. On the stairs, we pass the butcher's wife, Rosa. Twitching in a state of perpetual startlement, she sweats anxiety, drifting from apology to apology; compulsively rubbing her hands on her work smock because she's dirty somehow. But it's painted all over her. Plump, a cotton apron with a dandelion pattern. She's a sack full of market vegetables, a distinct smell of raw lamb chops. An angry aubergine under her left eye makes her squint and hide it with her hair. Her fingers tremor lightly like her lips when she feigns to smile. The butcher's a cunt.

We say the word, *cunt,* out loud, softly. The word bypasses me in the mind, an expletive vomited up from the gut. It is just quietly under our breath, but Rosa must hear it, at least we think she does. She keeps walking, avoiding the language of violence. She has heard it before. We turn and see the butcher's wife's backside trumping up the stairs to the broom closet, her steatopygous form. Two cauliflowers dancing behind a linen sheet. Just like our mother T. Do you remember?

***

She was standing in the kitchen, stirring the bubbling soup, her body packed up, hunched over in a floral dress she bought at the thrift store. She smelt different then, like the soup itself: barley, ham, fresh vegetables, onion, sweat. She'd let us take a taste from the ladle and she snorted when the soup burnt our top lip, because she knew that would happen. And we laughed a little bit, flushed with embarrassment and the safety of the love of our mother. But she didn't always show her love for us. She'd given it all away, had it sucked out, the flesh of her soul, drained through a tube and passed around to men with fifteen dollars an hour. It was all she had left after father got lost in the jungle, tangled in the vines. Top of the stairs, the door ajar, dull light seeping into the stairwell. A mournful violin seeped out of my bedroom door across the upstairs walkway. Our mother was half dead, curled up on the bed, with filthy hair, a piss-stained night dress. The blanket was on the floor 'cause she was running hot, no food or water in days. We sat on the edge of the bed, as if it were a lifeboat marooned on a grey shoal, looking at our mother ravaged by the swells of her psychosis. And we rubbed the back of her hand; her fingers were black and her nails were crags, chipped and torn. She felt our hand and rolled over. And the smell: urine, shit, sweat, damp. She was sinking into the air, rotting away in the bed, being lowered into a grave. But she cared for us, do you remember T.? When she wasn't sick, the ghoulish men and boys would pay the bills and she would cook for us, brush our hair, send us to school, until it was time for us to get a job and leave her alone with her soup and her sickness.

***

At the bottom of the stairs, out on the street, the butcher shop window is a meat aquarium, dull blue, filled with sea water and full of specimens of leg and shank, sausage and shoulder, all arranged with toothpicks and prices, lamb legs and pig's heads hanging from hooks in the roof. We can hear it bubbling and popping away, if we listen carefully. Through the meat – the butcher, *sullenly… heavily…* lowers the meat cleaver, again, and again, a brute in a filthy apron, a boar head protruding from his collar, the back of the neck swollen and pocked with pimples and ingrown hairs. He raises the cleaver, but through the hanging meat display, his eyes stare out toward the street, sending out this threatening air, through the glass and into our lungs. We can breathe it in, this toxicity. There's just enough oxygen in it to keep us alive. Our eyes meet the butcher's for a moment.

Cunt – but we don't say it this time, not out loud.

***

It was music that saved us, at night in our room, mother

already with a punter or in a comatose sleep. It opened us up to a world of sound, all around us, the clanking of the train as it rolled by our front window, the thin wisp of traffic from the main road. It was a three-dimensional world of sound that we translated into musical notation in our mind, the dynamics adding shape and form to the world around us. It wasn't long until we heard the articulation of sound everywhere: the shuffling of feet on the street, the garbled voices of shop assistants and their customers. We borrowed manuscripts from the public library, notating the more interesting parts late at night, finding new ideas for our own original compositions. I suppose this is when the voices started. They would speak in surround sound in whispers and sometimes shouts. Annotating them was difficult, but with time we found ways to score them on the page, a private world that kept us safe, at least for a time.

The bully boys... Boar heads on them too. Or snake heads. Or wolves, bears, spiders. They grunted and guffawed. They pulled their dicks, and each other's when no one was watching. Measured them. Compared sizes. They would pin us down, sit on our chest, pull off our shirt, our pants, spit in our eyes. They would fondle us like we were a woman, roughly kneading our breasts, squeezing our buttocks, putting their dirty fingers in our mouths. They were cackling hyenas dripping spit from their jagged jaws, pouring our bag out in the dirt and pissing in it. They would punch and pinch and scratch (just having a laugh) and they stole our identity, pissing on it like everything else. They raped us. And there was nothing to be done… Until we left and put ourselves back together. They were the sound of mocking laughter, the crunch of goosestepping boots. Even in a civilised world, the barbarians rule. They pillage your identity. They are inbred. They all smell the same, of onions and meat that's just turning. Or maybe they are all ruled by the same maleficent mind. The slow rise of the meat cleaver. The electrified eyeballs, never blinking, buzz saws carving another identity, breaking it down and selling it off as offal in the shop window.

***

The factory is a working body, each section performing a different duty, keeping the whole alive. It splurts and cracks and twists and winds. Metal scrapes metal as the inner workings of foreign machinery slide through the chutes, the intestines, and into the hands of the workers. The machines are the organs, the heart, the liver, the kidneys. It all thrashes into a great cacophony, the collision of rhythms and percussion. We hear it coming together, a great capitalist symphony of drums and incidental noise. And the managers look on, behind the safety of bomb proof plexiglass, shuffling the paperwork and barking orders through the office door. "T.? My office!" The boss beckons with a short gesture and grunt. Late two days this week. She won't be happy. The office is a cool pool of sludge and turbid puddles, mud walls punctuated with pictures of factory execs and trophies for improved productivity. The squelch of mud gets stuck in our ears and the ooze works its way into our shoes, sodden socks riding up between our toes. *In the shit now!* Should have brought galoshes. The boss, a badger or a beaver or a platypus. Shiny hair. Wide rimmed glasses. Shitty muck drips from the ceiling onto the papers on the desk, the platypus' shoulders and thick neck. And next to her, the ambulance workers: burly men, bouncers, blonde bully boys, hospital soldiers with trunks for arms made for wrestling to the ground, incapacitating, whispering "shh… shh…" as they muzzle you, humiliating the fight out of you.

The platypus folds her fat fingers and squeezes them together. "How are you T.?" The office fills with the stink mud of condescension.

"I'm ok?"

"Ok… well, we need you to take a test." She looks up at the bully boys, securing their complicity.

"Why? What kind of test?" The water is rising, the banks of the office filling up with the murky river water. We'll drown if this keeps up.

"We need… a doctor needs to say you're okay for work." She smacks her platypus bill looking to end the conversation.

"Why wouldn't I be okay for work?" The filthy water is around our knees, moving up our legs. We can't shuffle our feet, rooted to the riverbed in front of the platypus queen.

"You were flagged, T…. It's just procedure." She's becoming impatient, the thin veil of condescension falling, revealing the platypus smirk that she's been trying to hide since we got in this mud hole.

"Flagged? For what!?" We scoff.

"Certain behaviours, tardiness, appearance. I don't want to go into it with you now." She taps the desk with her synthetic nail… tick-tick-tick… and averts her eyes.

"I'm not going. You can't make me. This is..!" An outrage, we were going to say. An outrage. We shoot a look at the bully boys. They take a step forward.

"Don't make a fuss, T. It'll be done in a few hours, and you'll back in no time."

So, the office is heavy with the weight of mud now, the banks of the platypus' river dwelling swelling, the mud reaching our chin, our mouth. The mud's filling up our throat and we can't breathe. Mud splutter and we're crying filthy platypus tears. The muddy banks of the river pin our arms back, and we're helpless.

"You either walk out, or our friends here can carry you out." The platypus has stood up from her desk, the fur of her belly glistening in the dead brown water.

We have to submit, let go or we'll die in the grubby office with the soulless water born creature and her bully boys dressed as ambulance workers. Submit. Let go. The water recedes. The boys take our arm and lead us out, squelching in the muddy carpet, through the office door. The factory workers look up and the machines keep whirring away. But they only look for a second and put their eyes back on the machines. Productivity awards. The factory family. The bully boys strap me onto a bed in the back of the ambulance and ride up front without a word. We can't see out the window or hear above the motor's revving and the monstrous crunch of the gears. We are isolated to prevent spreading the infection.

***

It's cold and white in the robot womb with the doctor in his chair spinning across with a great big smile on his face. His hands are soft and pink. He's a fleshy robot too, his face all mottled with a lush white beard that he grooms in between consultations in the vanity mirror on his desk. There is a hum emanating from the bowels of the building, a constant drone suspending time and space. The room is just one small part of a much bigger organism. The doctor gestures for us to sit. Our mouth, our lips, our face, are all still caked with the platypus mud and the air is choked in the robot freezer. The doctor has veneers in that toothy grin, and they beam white spotlights, flashing strobes across our eyeballs. He's as fake as they come. And he's dangerous. We just know. We've met men like this before.

"How are you feeling, T.?" His voice is thin, metallic. Odd from such a fleshy body. They must have caked on fat and viscera to the robot scaffold, aluminium spine and cold jelly rubber synapses.

"Why am I here?"

"Why do you think you are here?"

"They said I need a test."

"Yes, well… We'll come to that." He's still grinning high beam veneers. "How would you rate your mood… out of ten?"

"Out of ten? Ten! I feel fucking great."

"Good. Well, that's good. Your workplace is… concerned. Maybe you can tell me why?"

"I have no idea. I was late a couple of times, that's all."

"You see, T., society has a certain expectation of us. The way we function, present, comply. Do you think you're meeting expectations?"

We offer a weak smile and a shrug.

"Mental hygiene is the trick, T. Sanitising the mind. Cleaning out the undesirables, the crude thoughts, violent thoughts, anything that makes you a bad 'mental citizen'."

So, he buzzes on much the same, his little whiny, artificial voice spinning out clichés and jargon. He has an image of a brain that he points to with a pencil, circling different areas that need to be cleansed. And then he pulls out cards with pictures on them. "A Rorschach test of sorts." He smiles.

First card: An empty stave, oozing infection

Second: the impressionistic, roadkill body of a disarticulated cello

Third: a grand piano with an axe in it, metallic strings and flying padded hammers, a cracked zombie cantaloupe

But we don't tell him these things, T. We just say, "A mill next to a serene stream with a lovely little bridge. A wedding day, with floating butterflies and doves released high into the ocean sky. Puppies. Unicorns. Rainbows. No broken knuckles or snapped fibulas, no." When he's done, they take us to a room with a bed, a toilet, and a sink. And it's the inside of a spaceship cruise with everything in its right place. The sound envelopes us, a warm digital drone in the bass register. An electronic ambience. It is a spaceship full of zombie rats, like us. Greasy hair, dirty fingers, sweat and shit on their clothes, all in the pristine starship headed deep into space, with no plan to return. Just space junk shot into the darkness, so we don't muck up the earth. It doesn't take long, and the bully boys are back.

"Doctor says you might be here a while. You need to take this." He holds up a wet syringe.

"I'm not taking that!" And we mean it. We fight them right down to the ground, but they sit on our back and put a shin in our neck as they penetrate us… a quivering, eager needle. And we are the punching bag taking on the world. Probed. A barrage of tests. Walking around in circles in the assembly area, stinking of piss, without a mind on the rudder. Until… *days…? weeks…? months…?* the doctor says we can go.

"Whatever you do, don't stop taking the medication suddenly." A detached voice, out of sync with the lopsided lips, suspended in space.

Back to the real world with a paper bag full of poison and the slippers they let you keep.

Sweaty stained sheets, and the window cracked to let in the stink of the street. And I tell you T., we're not taking that poison medication they gave us, no fucking way. But the kick back is hard. More than we expected. We both suffer in different ways, mind and body.

***

Dreams now... rolling in deep space, angelic bodies illuminated through touch. Golden fingers, purity and the resonance of astral harmony keeping us suspended in the womb of the universe. But the black balloon of the dark matter bursts, the stars exploding in distant galaxies… pop… pop… cheaply made, illegal fireworks misfiring and skating over the roof of the building and into the street. All things must end, and the plug of the sink comes loose, the universe spiralling into the drain of another reality. The sound of a distant orchestra reverberates around our skull, its transcendental, rampant harmonies bleeding from our ears. Cramping hard, doubled over a calcified toilet bowl, the glorious eruption of a wisdom tooth covered in plaque. Our body is quaking. A grinning mouth of vomit on the edge of the bed, dripping out onto the floor and shaking under the weight of a seismic event. Shaking… violently shaking.

Five days in our own shit, rolling over and over, the bed's a black hole sucking us up: the sheets, the room, the window imploding and the street reeling through, the brick buildings spinning in the vortex of the blackened mattress, the butcher's shop, the knives slashing in the air, the meat slapping against the bed frame, the factory pulled through, machines clanking down the sides of the gravity well, the countryside, cows, sheep, farmers with antique pipes, tractors, barren trees stripped of their leaves, and further out, the blue sky of midday, then the night sky, the moon clogging the vacuum momentarily and the stars exploding as they rip through time and space.

***

Five days without the doctor's medication. It's the poison that cuts a rift between us, me and you, T. And Rosa comes with soup when she can get away from the butcher, quietly closing the door behind her without a word. It is enough, the soup and the tap water, to sustain us, although we shit it out and vomit it up, sweat it through our filthy pores. But by the fifth day we can sit up on the edge of the bed with our head in our hands and think straight. Straight enough that we know we have been reunited, you and I, mind and body, the master and the puppet. The smell is overpowering, a human in decay, shedding viscera, hair greased up with scalp oil and the sallow skin on our arms and legs, skeletal frame emaciated by the drug fever. But we are in it together, you and me. A knock at the door and the smell of soup. We roll over to face the wall and we hear a bowl clink and come to rest down on the ground by the bed. The door shuts quietly.

"Mildred?" We are lost somewhere here. Let's go back to a story we both remember.

***

Mildred was a meerkat: sleek, firm, inquisitive. She lived in a rundown burrow on the outskirts of the city, next to a rail bridge where the streetlamps dripped light into the gutters, a sallow bile. Beckoning from her room, her forgotten theme, a string quartet playing quietly calling us in. Her room was packed in with all the other girls behind thin walls, the music playing to drown out the sounds of desperate, drunk men pounding the bed heads like the booming of a jack hammer on a work site. We went there for respite. A place to hide intentionally from the anxiety, the submission and humiliation of the factory, the platypus and the butcher in the window with his cleaver. We didn't speak at first. She took off our shoes and socks, washed our feet in perfumed water, running her hands up our calves, past our knees to our thighs. Her loose blouse would dangle invitingly open exposing her hard breasts and erect nipples in the cold air of the night, all by the red light of the covered lamp by her bedside. We couldn't give over to it, not completely. We were always the 'other', T., our body, our cracked feet, cragged toenails, the body of something already dead, too far gone. For Millie, nothing more than a sick pet, easy money. We came back time and again, always leaving a little extra cash on the bedside table when we left. On these nights we would sometimes stay until morning, just lying in Millie's arms, her tight stomach pressed against ours, her fingers tracing around our cheeks, across our chin and jaw, around our ears. She knew what we wanted. Not a cheap, hard fuck against the wall. It was compassion, tenderness, that we paid for. It was the unburdening of moral judgment that we experienced at the point of asphyxiation and orgasm. And after a while the connection between us blossomed into a kind of distorted love burping in the clogged aorta of our heart. We knew for sure we loved her when we heard her sing. She would hum quietly when she held us in her arms, running her fingers down our arm.

"Do you love me, Millie?" we asked.

She scoffed, "You don't pay me enough."

"I love you." The words dropped out of our mouth, fat drops of rain that arrive unannounced on a summer afternoon.

"I know you do, T. You got to save some of that love for yourself."

The words felt cheap, like we got what we paid for. Anyway, it was enough to make us believe until the next time. But there was no next time, not for us. Sleet on the pavement under the bridge, the lamp post flickering shards of light in and out of the darkness. The warren was busy. Punters and the meerkat girls holding them up, disappearing behind closed doors and into dimly lit rooms. Her room was the same, but it was a different meerkat sitting on the bed, waiting for a customer, waiting to start the act all over again. She was beautiful, with a mane of red hair falling over her naked breasts and she pasted on a smile for when she saw us. But she was not Millie. Her essence, her temperature was different, her heartbeat at a slower rate and we knew she was too far lost in the world of the warren to understand compassion or love or respite.

"Where's Mildred? Where's Mildred?"

The poor girl looked startled. "Mildred? There's no one here by that name, love."

We knew she was gone into the ether, or on a greyhound. On a rocket ship to establish a new utopia. Maybe she was just lifeless, floating in the river by the factory where no one would be looking for her, no one would find her. So, we walked on into the sleet and the beginnings of the snow buffeting our face, catching our hair. The wind was running chills through our cheeks and down our arms, into our fingers, arthritic with the cold. Back to the butcher's, back to the apartment to sleep on our side alone, dreaming of Millie's fingers in our hair, the string quartet dolefully playing her theme. She was the love of our life, and we paid by the hour.

Voices

There's a ghoul in the mirror!

Hollow cheeked...

Gossamer skin...

A wisp of steam...

Coma aberration lens...

Temporal deceleration...

The razor knicks the neck

We will leave this apartment today, T., take the air. Try to put it right. Out the door and down the steps, and there is Rosa, trumping her way up the stairs, two brass tuning slides opening and closing. She says nothing. Her face speaks for her. The aubergine under the eye now, framed with a yellow and black ring. Her other eye is pink and fleshy, pinched in, a swollen pork chop battered by the butcher's mallet. And when she tries to smile, she grimaces a little as her bottom lip, torn and split, rubs against her teeth. A red mist fills the staircase, and you hand over the reins to me, T. A mind, flooded with rage. All the bully boys flashing before us. It's finally time. *Do something!* The kitchen knife is by the sink in the apartment. Down the stairs – no rush – we adjust our coat collar. Out into the street, and he's there, the butcher in the window, the cleaver in his hand. *Tap… tap…* the butt of the knife on the window. His eyes are staring, a maniacal emptiness, another void, sucking in the street, drawing us in. He's not laughing, just… just emptiness. Wiping his hooves on his apron, he walks outside, purposefully towards us. And there is the shop and the street, the sky flickering and faltering, the buildings bowing, the whole world in a spy glass. We're breathing hard, chest rising and falling, full of hot air, a boy facing his Goliath. The butcher's hand reaches out in slow motion, waves of eternity rippling through the air, the shop window bending, warped by the inconsistency of time. All the bully boys, the boar's heads, all standing in front of us, the alphas turning the world over in their swollen fists. We are in perfect synergy, you and I, T. The mind that fills with hate; the hands that succumb to the impulse. Can you hear it? The madness in the music now. *Whip… lash…* and the boar head screams. The knife goes in hard, catching the belt buckle on the first thrust, but we shank him again and again. *Yes, T.! We're doing it!* The fat fuck is punctured, compromised. His gut is oozing and swelling up, blood and grey sludge pouring out. The whole world is watching us, this our greatest performance, our greatest composition, our service to humanity, to Rosa. We're fucking him, T.! Fucking him with our bloody hands, this knife! And the pain! Can you feel it, T.? Oh, I can feel it. Gorgeous pain, in his eyes, his crippled hands, his gut, his mind ravaged by it, the emptiness in his eyes filled with rich gushes of pain! We're doing it, T.! We're really doing it! In and out as easy as cutlery in a drawer.

Carve him up, T! This bastard animal. *He deserves it, they all deserve it!* The butcher's grabbing our arms, but he's too far gone and he's falling fast. Crumbling in slow motion, a demolished building, onto his knees and we're wrestling with him until the fight is gone and he's limp on the pavement. *Now we finish it, T.* We drive the knife into his eye as he sputters and gurgles his last. The eye's a supernova exploding, and it's done.

"Like a pig! Like a pig in the street!" we howl, the pavement now full of bystanders, mothers with their children in prams, terrified, stunted in time. And a glorious eruption of music! Can you hear it T., blasting from the heavens, covering the street in dissonance and destruction? In the shop window, hiding behind the aquarium of meat, Rosa holds her hands, quivering over her mouth. We lock eyes with her. Her expression is full of meaning, but none we can understand. It is over now, we try to tell her without words, but she runs to her husband, holding his lifeless body in her hands. She is wailing, uncontrollably. "What have you done?! Have you lost your mind?!" It's all she could think to say.

"Oh Rosa… My mind is finally free!" We wave the knife flamboyantly in the air.

Across the street, amongst the bystanders, an old woman cowers behind her shopping trolley. And she's in the care home a week later. *"And the pity of it all. It's just so sad."*

Autopilot… We sail down the street, across the bridge, over the river, robotically making our way to the factory with wayward strides, the bloody knife pointing down to the ground, an upturned baby bottle messing up the kitchen floor. We are dancing to a distorted waltz, swaying with each step we take. And we can smell her, the old platypus, the stench of condescension. We can taste the mud in our mouth, the ugly riverbank office behind the great machines of the factory, creating, shaping, cleaning the internal parts of life's minutiae. Our hands, our clothes, covered in blood, splattered all over our face and our hair. The life essence of the butcher pasted all over us. Standing outside the factory, catching our breath.

The sirens must have been blaring for some time, when the blue boys took us down to the ground, ripping the shoulder, poking the ribs, blinding the eyes with their rough gloves and the knife rattling along the concrete, a razorblade across a set of front teeth. A bomb went off and our ears were ringing. Or was it all in the mind? It's hard to tell. There was screaming below the pitch of the blast maybe. And I think that we were smiling when they put us in the back of the van.

Or

We wave the knife limply in front of him, his powerful hand catching our wrist, the blade clinking on the pavement harmlessly. Without the need of violence, the butcher lowers us to the ground and sits on our back, his

hairy pig tail sprouting up from his leather belt, the top of
his buttocks pressed against the back of our head.

Or

We roll over in the sodden sheets.

Or

We're staring at the dandelions.

Or

We are capricious twists of fiction.

***

*'Disarticulated Psychosis. Very dangerous for you and the
people around you. Probable cause — wilful non-compliance to the
proposed medical regime. We'll need to keep you here I'm afraid...
indefinitely.'*

Unwelcome Guests

The moonlight caught the shadows in the lanes

And thunder chased the silence through the town

Drought had cracked and broken all the drains

And stoops drooped low like mustached hanging frowns

Wake to fright, a plush-lined funeral hearse

The sickly turn had taken full effect

Friendship born of reason's broken curse

Brothers bound together in neglect

Our prelapsarian moment

A broken image, intrusive thought

Witness and perpetrator

Temporal dilation, demolition

Ran the gauntlet one more time

Sweaty palms and petty crimes

Woke up to the same old mess

Fractured dreams

Unwelcome guests

***

The rats on the spaceship scurry around us, dragging
their legs, their fur greased up with the sweat of the air, the
oozing of the medication out of the pores, the oppressive
heat of the air conditioning. The windows are sealed to keep
us from touching the air outside and it is blast proof glass
and the low whisper of the air from the vents keeps
everything in a perpetual stasis. Bully boys at the doors
sometimes push us around in wheelchairs and the din of the
television's always on, disorganising our thoughts, the manic
sound disrupting our processes. Across the room, one of the
rats organises the magazines, the sketch books, the crayons,
systematically, only in a way she can understand. But she's
getting more and more manic with it, it's riling her up. She
throws a plastic mug full of coffee against the wall and pulls

her hair out all over the floor. And they're on her, the bully boys. The syringe is out, spluttering enthusiastically. She's limp on the floor when the gurney comes, and they wheel her away to strap her down until she's suitably sane. We're right here, T. This is today, or maybe yesterday or the day before. But it's today. We're right here. Why don't you just wake up so we can get the fuck out of here?!

***

Amoebans

Birds smack crudely against the window… flashes of lightning and a din of shouts, a pack of seagulls in the garden. *Wake up, T. We've got company!* The thump of a marching band booms in our ears, an alarm clock sending electric shocks through our brain. The front doors open, and the shouting reporters take a smoke break as the whisps of figures move around the front desk. Beeps from the security door to the patient lounge… *something's coming, T.! Something's happening…* A tall monument in a silk white skirt, blouse and suit jacket – powerful shoulder pads adding a masculine shape to her upper body – swaggers into the room, the rats all scurrying to the corners. Blonde hair, shoulder length and cut in a fringe, straightened with a carving knife. No hint of a smile on her face. Just big black eyes, worm holes or toilet bowls you circle down and get lost in a far-off galaxy. Those eyes would bleed black when she cried, and her blood would be blue and her shit would be neon green. She is a foreigner, to this facility, to this time, to this planet. She walks like a workman in heels too, leaning heavily side to side, her strong calves the foundations of her birthing hips. It's so easy, T., to judge a woman by her body. But sometimes you just don't know quite what you're looking at, when they're infinite genders in one. It makes my misogyny quiver. But who am I to judge? I'm a figment of the mind – bodiless, formless. My sexuality, my gender is all based on the impulses, the form you give me, T. Without you, maybe I would be androgenous. So, a pack of bully boys in black suits, with microphones and headphones hanging out their ears, all hooked up, holstered guns shifting out of their suit jackets. And their talking to someone in those headsets. Telling their own stories. The robot doctor walks in with his waxy beard, smiling those bright veneers and fussing around the woman in white. *Something is going down here…*

"Are they all here permanently, Doctor?" Her lips move out of time with the words, like her body is a substitute for a greater power. She walks slowly around the room – past the rat playing connect four on his own, the fat one with yogurt all over his face, the one combing the knots out of her grey, toast dry hair, weaving a hair rug on her lap and across the floor.

"Uh… no, Minister. We aim to reintegrate most of them into society, once they are properly tuned to society's expectations…"

She looks thoughtfully out the window for a moment at the seagull reporters, at the dandelions. Something is passing through her mind, something eternal. And her black eyes look out across the room, wormholes spinning right into our eyes, T. We've been made. She's looking right through you and straight at me. Past the body, into the mind. I can feel her moving around in here. Running her fingers across the dusty furniture. Straightening the picture frames.

"And this one? Why is he here?" She is towering over us, a massive skyscraper in the business district, a popular suicide destination, and I can feel the acrophobia rising as we scale the obscure glass windows, the white cement girders, and reach back inside the worm holes in her expressionless face.

"Oh… he is a… special case, Minister. Not someone you should worry about…" The doctor tries to usher her on by the arm, but she flinches and the bully boy security inch forward.

"Please Doctor, tell me why he is here." No hint of impatience in her voice. No hint of emotion.

"Uh… disarticulated psychosis, Minister." The doctor waits for a response but the woman in white is unmoved, waiting for a further explanation. "Right, well… He's been disentangled from his identity." The doctor was struggling to find a way to explain it. "…it's relatively new in the literature, you see. Uh…his mind is a separate entity to him as a person… his physical self… his body. Violent thoughts… lude cravings… a profligate lifestyle." The woman in white plays with her polished nails.

"His mind is unclean, Minister. We are trying to unite him with his true self… the one fit for society."

Or

"He's a maniac! A fucking psychopath! Don't touch him! You'll never get the stink off!"

The woman in white is intrigued, though. "Hmmm… I would like to know how that feels, doctor. That is why I am here after all. To put myself in the skin, if you like, of the patients you have here."

"Oh no… Forgive me for saying, but it would be a bad idea, Minister. Congress with such a disturbed mind might have adverse effects on you…"

Or

"He'll twist you up that fucker! You'll never be the

same…"

The impression of a wry smile on the woman's face. "I think I can handle it, doctor."

The bully boys pin us down again, T. Take our plastic pants off. Spread our legs. Wrestling, thrashing. Coming to rest. Finally submitting. And something has possessed the woman in white. She is shaking, her knees buckling. And I knew it, T. There was something about her. She just didn't look herself. A blue gelatinous mass slides out the bottom of the woman's dress, her crumpled, lifeless body falling to the floor, a sack of distended joints and flaccid limbs. An Amoeban! A real Amoeban! Not a woman at all. We've never met one, but I could pick one out in their host skin suit a mile away. Sliding across the floor, they come for us, and we wrestle again, our cock exposed, our ass spread apart. It's cold, T., on our legs and up our thighs… and they're an ox tongue licking at our asshole, worming their way inside us. So cold and dense. The initial pain as they penetrate us, the Amoeban working their way through our intestines, up, through and out, clamping around our nervous system, reaching a cold globular finger around our brainstem. And it's an ocean of blue inside our head, I know you can't see it, T., but they're here, occupying our brain, panzers over the Ukrainian border, blowing holes in synapses, taking the frontal lobe and working back. We are powerless under the Amoeban control. Floating in a jar, conversing telepathically with this malignant tumour.

***

"What the fuck is happening?"

> *"Please don't be alarmed. I promise, this is only a fleeting visit. I am just here to see things from your perspective… get inside your head for a while."*

"Why? Why the fuck would you want to do that?"

> *"You see, I'm the Minister for Mental Health it's my duty to*

I'm to visit the high security wards across the country. I need to make sure we have you in the right place."

"The right place? You must be joking!

These doctors, they keep us drugged up

on this medication so we can't move,

or think straight… They are censors of the soul, filtering out the

depraved, the debaucherous, the truth, the humanity!"

"Oh God, I could be bounded
in a nutshell, and count myself
a king of infinite space, were it
not that I have bad dreams."

"What?!"

'Nothing, dear. Anyway,
surely this is for your own good?

They say you are

disarticulated."

"Look… all I am guilty of is being free of mind. I

work in dreams, memories, fictions. If that is illegal,

then we are all prisoners, our thoughts locked behind a

wall of sensibility."

*"I see… Well said. But this is
your story, surely anything is
possible."*

She pauses for a moment, lets

this sink in.

"Well, it seems limitless in here.

Technically you live inside me now both figuratively and literally.

Perhaps you're my creation, I could send you out into the vacuum of

deep space, and watch your globular mass carve apart under the

pressure." "Blow winds, and crack your cheeks! Rage! Blow!", I

like this. Finally, a host worthy of my visitation. I want to know

one more thing before I go… are you an unclean mind? Do you

need to be

'rehabilitated'?"

"Honestly? I am pure filth, Minister.

I am a towering edifice, sublime in its magnitude, seated

high up, beyond the radar of society's expectations,

breaking the slimy stratosphere of censorship and

control. I am a gaping mind flooded with impure

thoughts, violence, sexual destruction, misogyny. I am

a butcher's knife in the viscera but only because that is

what you ordered.

And there is such sweet music here in this internal world,

grand orchestras of sound, nature's soundtrack bellowing above the
skyline.

In the external world, they are merely whimpers, muted trombones,

tuning slides sadly accompanying the disappointment of reality.

In here, I am the composer, I am life. I am death. I am God, Minister.

Impervious to the doctor's chemical straight jacket."

"No… I think not. You, it
seems to me, you are merely an
agent provocateur, a crude mind

*with a megaphone, but without
an audience. You are an empty
prophet. You see, I know God.
I pray to him at night, a kind
of self-flagellation… begging
forgiveness for my
transgressions. I pray at the foot
of my bed by a wooden log that
I strap my host body to. The
guards strap her back with thin
whips and beat her with heavy
clubs until the body finally
submits and I leave her to rest,
prostate and bloody across the
log. I do not feel the pain, you
see. I just know that it is being
inflicted, and I feel, somehow,
better. And you. What will we
do with you? 'Madness in great
ones should not unwatched go.'
But, no, you are not a great
one. You are not God, and you
are foolish for thinking so. God
is genderless, sexless. God is
merciless, compassionless. Eons*

"Is that all you think I am, Minister?"

***

And the clamp around our spine is loosened, T. You can feel it, right? They are leaving us, sliding through our organs and down our intestinal tract. A burst from the anus, blue gloop protruding from our asshole and they are out in the air again. We are empty and free. From the floor, we can see them returning to their host body, up through the slip of the dress, past the knees. The body takes on life and they are returned to their chosen identity. 'They' are a 'she' once more. And soon, she is outside, in the flock of camera flashes, making statements, taking questions. The hidden Amoeban in the coat of flesh and viscera, straddling their portfolio like a colossus.

But we can't get the blue ocean out of our eyes for days, T. We are swimming in it. The doctor says it is not unusual… just a case of telepathic cynopsia. He says it will pass. Everything is under water, the spaceship facility, the garden through the bulletproof glass. We toss and turn at night in a fish tank, locked in, drowning. That minister left a part of themselves, mycelium roots, a telepathic network, slender threads reaching back to the source. And we can't get the sound out of our ears, the droning, the persistent laconic theme. And we are visited by the Amoeban, in our

memories, in our dreams. They left a part of themselves inside us T., maybe an infection, spread through the neural pathways, affecting us both, mind and body. Maybe just a place card, identifying their place in the world. I feel their story moving in us. We are becoming them, floating in their globular sea of Amoebans, splitting the nucleus, the cytoplasm. Binary fission. An exact replica of the Minister floating through our neurotransmitters. Taking over our frontal lobe, our amygdala. And now we are androgenous, amorphic. We feel the lassitude of an absence of gender, then a collision of endless sexual identities, shattered kaleidoscopic vision, the possibilities of telepathic genitalia. We can reason that we are both nothing and everything all at once, limited to the mind, the body of little significance. And I feel one with the Amoebans, momentarily. But… there is a loss here, viscerally. It is as if fucking is in the realm of dreams and memory, not the palpitating heart, the rigid cock or dripping cunt. The pleasure imagined rather than experienced in the body. And how can it be imagined accurately, even in memory? We do not fondly remember sexual adventures without touching ourselves. Perhaps, there is a way only known to those who have never felt this kind of palpable, physical expression. The Amoebans must know it. I wish we had mind fucked that Amoeban, T. We might have learned of a depravity unknown to us, deeper and more satisfying. Should I submit? Let the Amoeban inhabit us? 'I' am 'they'…

Amoeban Echoes

Waves Pounding Against the Breaker... (a spurious autobiography)

Hanging in the crags of rock at the summit of the cove, a palatial mansion reached out over the cliff top, touching the glass face of the endless ocean. Macaws played in the rosewood trees and toucans, high on the mushrooms that shaded under the tree canopies, wound loosely by the runner plants around the pillars below the balcony. Small birds would swoop, as they took off with a beak full of the mushrooms' meat, and quickly dart away in fear of being eaten themselves. Servants, gardeners, cleaners and cooks. They all scurried about the property, mechanical mice on timers, loops, schedules. They would service parties for the Amoeban hosts, where the guests would sit in union with each other. Motionless, they would connect telepathically and imagine the most lavish parties ever created. Baths of French champagne, fountains of lemon gin and play pools filled with cocaine dust. And all around them the psylocibin of the glowing mushrooms from under the balcony.

The mycelium roots tangled around their amorphous bodies, connecting them together in a great hallucinogenic system of fibrous thread. Soon, *their minds would devolve into mass orgies, where pleasure was fired by the intellect, the groping synapses of sapiosexuals.*

[And we can feel it, T. The dusk of a million glistening neurons, the acidity of a sodden amygdala dipped in the champagne bath, the frontal cortex covered in the fountain gin… This story has promise…]

But these parties only live in my imagination. Just me living vicariously through my Amoeban friends' accounts: rumour and inuendo. I was too young to take part. The servants were never to know about this turgid inner world of the Amoebans. To them, the parties were sedate, boring affairs, with only the occasional need of lubrication. It was a hidden world, repressed, forbidden. But I felt it swelling in me, the need to explore myself, my sexuality. And the more it was taboo, the more I wanted to know about it. There was no gender to be attracted to, no body to idolise, sexualise. It began with thoughts, mind movies with little material to replicate.

So, it was a busy life, but it seemed an empty house, the vastness of the balcony, the inset dining area leading through to a myriad of spaces, bedrooms, sitting rooms, kitchens and laundries. It felt empty to me, at an age where I was old enough to reflect on the past but also perpetually living on the edge of the future. Perhaps always one step away from disaster. And, having lived so carefree in the world, it was only now that I was coming to terms with my identity, my place in society. It was an awakening, the realisation of the form of my body, the workings of my mind. These had not been separate before in my younger years. Speech was always through the mind: touch and sensation not hindered by pleasure or pain. These were lessons that I learned in the mind alone. And I was lonely. Even as an Amoeban, I never felt like I truly fitted in. So, it was not at all strange that I had found somebody, a young human man, that I would explore these ideas with, pleasure and pain. We were the same age, on the brink of university, sharing a passion for the classics, social justice, philosophy and politics. We would spend afternoons reciting Shakespeare and Milton, John Stuart Mill and Jeremy Bentham. It was naïve, ill fated, but it was a form of innocent love that I could not deny. The older generation did not believe in these things. Love was a fantasy, unnecessary for existence. Amoeban orgasms were fictional, adaptations of stories from other races that were tied to the vicissitudes of the body. Pain was cerebral. Something to inflict strategically. Psychic pain, wilful perpetrators of trauma without the invasion of the body, the tearing of flesh. But I experimented, nonetheless, with my new friend, penetrating his mind and stupefying his fleshy body with thoughts of pain and pleasure. And it was the first time that I entered a human as a skin suit, expressly for the purpose of pleasure. In my lover's mind, he would communicate his desires, until a psychic moment of passion left him a wobbling mess, supine, staring at the chandeliers. And I felt satisfied for that moment, even in my youth, the luxury of the lifestyle, the complete lack of responsibility, the ripples of love and acceptance. It was a simple, yet opulent life. Mycelial ropes binding human flesh and brains, the *bondage of thoughts, desires, laced with psylocibin and Amoeban ooze. Desires finding their threshold in psychosis, hallucinogenic orgasms splurting out of ventricles, the warm semen of the mind, a rich plasmatic wave of endorphin. But, inevitably in the carelessness of youth, we were caught, the two psychic lovers lolling on the floor behind the bed by my creator, a dull-witted, Minister for Science. It was unseemly, grotesque, unscientific. It was bestiality! And it was illegal, telepathic sexual activity between the human and Amoeban race. Something impure. I was sent away to the city, far from the seaside home I had become accustomed to. Far from the passionate thoughts of my newfound lover that occupied my mind.*

[Can you hear me, T.? I'm not lost. I'm still here. The waves of rippling cytoplasm keep coming. Brace yourself!]

Throughout university, I was the only one of my kind. I would look around at the sea of skin, bone, fat, hair, eyeballs, fingernails, beards, cleavage, and just see the otherness; the difference between the Amoeban form and the slabs of malformed meat. For years, I felt isolated, unable to communicate. Lecturers found it difficult to pass on important information, and other students laughed behind my back (although it was unclear there was a front or back in Amoeban anatomy). Boys and girls would invite me to parties, get me drunk, and unload their filthy desires in a telepathic relay. And I succumbed, sharing what I had learnt with my lover back home, with the drunken louts in the student accommodation. I became infamous, the mind fuck Amoeban, blowing the tops off imagined cocks and leaving their girlfriends writhing in psychic pleasure. By the end of university, I had amassed a set of middling grades, and a reputation as the androgenous Amoeban slut. But Amoebans are never as hospitable as people presume.

There is always an angle, a play, that ends with the downfall of our enemies. It must first be learned, this tactical position, through the experience of treachery and violence perpetrated by our human counterparts. And what these humans didn't know was very dangerous indeed. For each encounter, each mind fuck, I had left a little present behind, a farewell gift.

Soon the campus was rife with fevered brains and psychotic behaviours. Students masturbating frantically in front of the conservatorium, in lectures and tutorials. They were tearing at their clothes, their dresses, exposing themselves to strangers on the street. Frat boys defecating into their hands and wiping shit across their brows, their lips, their chests. And for some poor souls, the endless orgasm: a windup soldier fallen sideways, turning in endless circles, seeped in a pool of ectoplasm. Amoeban Syphilis. Malignant. Sexual Terrorism. Spread like wild fire from a single source.

[Everything is vibrating, T. It's the moment when pleasure becomes a raw, compulsive action. Are we infected?

Amoeban syphilis?]

Politics was easy for me after that. The competition had been eradicated. The experience at Unversity had hardened me, helped me to see the depraved desires of others. I became proud of my appearance, boldly flaunting my Amoeban form at workplaces and at parties. It wasn't until I ran for Health Minister that I adopted the skin suit host again, hiding my identity in the clothes of party politics forever. Underneath, I remained, pulling the strings. But I was an embittered servant to the city, a damaged mind that suspected the worst in others and planned their demise. I was a survivor. I knew myself entirely. It was then that I had become a true Amoeban…

[T.? Are you still there? The blue is rising. I can see, even in the dark room. Those Amoebans are tough. A race of globular, amorphous beings. Androgenous. Self-fertilizing. Telepathic. They're a lot like us, disarticulated at first, trying to find their true selves. Those doctors, society's expectations. We could be Amoeban, T., if our story took a different turn. Close your eyes. We need our rest. The last thing we need tonight is another mind fuck…]

Snakes

Snakes! Can you feel that dead, fleshy weight on our leg, T.? It's inching up our ankle, slowly, methodically. The celesta above the untuned percussion of the orchestra, creeping in slowly, waiting, poised to strike. They're searching for the hole in the knee of our trousers, and then inside it's jelly, soft, frozen jelly working its way up our thigh, into our underwear, searching out the warmth, wrapping around our scrotum. And you better not move T., because you know what this is? It's an infestation of our body, a paralysing fear hypnotising the mind. It's a slithering, scaled projection of the nightmare we've found ourselves in. *It's fucking snakes, T.! Don't fucking move!*

***

"Electric impulses in the extremities at first, then full movement of the fingers and toes. A slow return, a reanimation of the legs, the muscles rigid and twitching. Then the arms: rotation of the shoulders, bending of the elbows. Finally, the neck twisting right to left, left to right. And you're newborn. You're back with us." The doctor thinks the medication is settling, being absorbed, metabolised by the body.

Now, you're playing connect four, reading the complimentary Reader's Digest, touching yourself with vigour again in the shower, T. And I'll let you be, for now, let you do your thing. They've even got you helping out at mealtimes: cleaning up the plastic plates, the cutlery, packing up the trays. But they won't let you near the kitchen, not near the knives, the pots and pans, the burner flames of the gas stove. Not near the garbage disposal, in case you jam a fist into it. Not near the oven, in case you decide to gas us both or blow up the whole fucking facility. And the rats are paying attention to our reanimation. Their talking to us, a million stories at once, playing cards with a deck and no aces. And we are sitting quietly, considering the dandelions with a cup of tea. It's a rest home now, and it's *fucking boring*. So boring, it's dangerous. The monotonous repetition of predictable melodies. The mindless lyrics of popstars playing on the radio. We'll get some twisted ideas if we're left to rot in here. *Sensory deprivation! Mental starvation! Atrophy of the mind and the body!* At least there's Mal prancing around to keep us entertained. He has the most grotesque smile, like he's painted it on, and he wears women's stockings, bright yellow fishnets. They made him put his pants back over them, but he rolls up his trousers, lets everyone know he's wearing them. Dancing and smiling, a real maniac, up, up and away like the world's a playground in a cloud up to heaven. When he gets too high, the bully boys lock him in a dark room to settle down. We're used to him floating in and out spreading his distorted love around the room.

The tv drones on and on, twenty-four-hour news, or tugging the game show puppets, making them laugh, making them smile. Public service announcements, reptilian philosopher kings doing what's best for the nation. Ringing in the ears, the synapses. Raw brain meat from the numbness of the facility. Reality tv, wax mannequins with exploded cheek bones from being injected with a punch in the face. Courting, flirting, kissing, but they keep the fucking a secret so the kids can watch. The news anchor talks to us sometimes, giving us hints on moral and ethical issues. Wars and famines. Which side to vote for. Imperialist television. Pestilence, drought, floods, cyclones. There's an interview with the old woman on the street – socially conscious bystander – *"And the pity of it all. It's just so sad."* Paedophiles, rapists, murderers. Shock and indignation. Something to throw a shoe at. At least we've got a paper and pencil, something to annotate the sounds around us. It's not so bad playing by ourselves.

***

And now there is Viktor. He introduces himself, the big lump with wide shoulders and a crew cut. A slab of county fresh beef from the farm. He wanders in and out, in the periphery. Then, magic… he's on us. And always with the questions, requests.

"Can you get me a new pair of galoshes next time you're out?"

Or

"I smoke the blues. The reds are too harsh. Get me a pack next time you're at the store."

Or

"I've got to tell you, I do feel low today. Maybe it's the weather. Get me a length of rope when you're at the hardware store?"

It has become clear; changes have been made to the facility. Client centred. Recovery based. Reintegration management. There's a pool table, ping pong, an upright piano, second hand massage chairs and an exercise bike. Holistic therapy sessions. African drumming circles. Finger painting. And there are fewer bully boys hovering over us. Less doctors too.

***

The factory life did not suit us. The horn blaring, signalling the start of our shift. The ding-dong announcements to increase productivity.

"You are important to us. You are part of the factory family."

And the platypus was on to us, all the days off after nights out with Mildred. The drinking on the job to stave off the boredom of repetition. The meat sticks bent in clawing machines — more days off. The ding in the forklift's bumper. The same shirt as yesterday, and the day before that. The sweat stains in the armpits, the stink of the regretful hangover. The mumbling to ourselves and the contained explosions of anger at co-workers. She was on to us alright. She'd leave her office just to look us up and down and then turn around and go back in. But everyone was too scared to bring up the obvious, our wilful denial of company policy.

Fuck the factory family! Fuck the platypus!

But there was always Mildred waiting at the end of the shift. And the factory paid for us to be together, even if they didn't know it. Sometimes suits would come in to look around. We saw them through the plexiglass those reptile fuckers, all shiny, slinking around with clipboards, snakes winding their way through the machinery, ignoring the common folk, making their way gradually up the corporate ladder.

We caught eyes with one of them, do you remember, T.? We were a poster on the wall. An inanimate object. A toaster. A coffee pot. We carved him up. Stuck him in the jigsaw cutter, snake pieces. Fried them in the break room. Passed them around to the workers as a workplace incentive.

Or

We barged in to the platypus' mud hit office, unbuckled our pants, took a shit on the desk.

Or

We hid in the toilet until the snakes were gone.

We weren't ready for the twists of our narrative just yet, were we, T? We still lived almost exclusively in the physical world, the literal, where workers were workers and suits would always be snakes.

***

Now, the bully boys are gone completely. One at a time, less and less of them, until we're sitting here staring at a beige wall, counting the chips in the paint, and there's no one here at all. It's just you and me T. For the first time since we got here, I can recognise a moment of solitude. There's a wisp of wind in the room too, where there shouldn't be, and we can smell the bog of the marshlands through an opening in the impenetrable facility walls. No one in the hallway. No one by the pool table. No one in the garden, smoking or counting dandelions. A revolving door is rotating in the wind, letting in the marsh, the breeze, the smell of freedom. *Do it, T. Do it, now!*

A few steps to freedom. Outside, the senses lift with the stench of fertiliser and tepid water. *Walk, T.!* Through the garden and the gate. Down the winding path to the bog. Through the grey water and the claws of the marsh trees drowned in the toxic bed of a dead river. And further out, through a pasture and a farmhouse, out to the highway, where cars are buzzing flies moving up and down the pane of glass. There is the wholesome stink of petrol as we dodge between the traffic, our white facility pyjamas clinging to our chest. And we can hear it all, T., a symphony of natural sound, one great field recording of the infinite details of life, the sounds evidence of existence. On the other side, in the distance, the city of sin, the boroughs, the dirty stoops, the vermin under the bridges, the butcher shop, the factory. But now that we're here, it looks like the butcher shop is gone. The meat aquarium is boarded up, the apartment window smashed, shards of glass lying on the pavement. Maybe it was always like this. Maybe we've been living in the future, and we didn't even know it. No butcher, no Rosa. No eccentric factory worker in the first-floor apartment. It's sad, what becomes of a broken past. Our hands are tired, worn out with all the drugs and the emaciation of incarceration. They're translucent pig's feet. We're turning invisible. The old woman on the street shuffles past with her shopping trolley and she almost knocks us over, like we've moved on from this realm into another dimension, another reality. Or maybe to no reality at all, just fading out of existence forever. The street is filled with the hoots of sirens, and the blaring of the blue boys' cars shooting past us, stirring up our hair and knocking us backward. But they don't see us, T. Maybe we're in the future. Maybe we're dead and gone, just an ethereal wisp of memory left echoing at the end of the story. *Pick up the shattered glass, T. Now run it across the palm of your hand. Can you feel that? That's real pain, impossible to imagine without being alive in the physical world. Let that be a reminder, T., a reminder that we're still alive.*

***

Autopilot... Back to the factory. The pain in our hand is throbbing, the bleeding worse than we expected. There is the corpse of a robotic sheep, twisted metal and ragged concrete slabs. Sheet metal skin tags cover the detritus of a riverbank office and a factory floor. No more factory. No more occupation. No more social identity. We head back through the city, walking through a crowd, pedestrians moving away from us. Some kind of reverse gravitational force is emanating from us. But the meerkat burrow is still there. We've got no money. We won't be able to buy some compassion today. And the bridge is still there, jutting out of the festering river. Maybe we should sit for a while, lie down. This hand is killing us. The hard cobbled path under the bridge, a torture chamber, clinging on to the wall of the bridge support. We lie like this, staring at a weed sprouting out of the pavement. The past, the present, the future. It all seems so far away now.

***

Night creeps in and so do the bridge trolls, setting up camp around us. It's freezing here. The wind whips under the breezeway, coming off the river, stinking of dead fish and missing persons. The bridge trolls are multiplying until there's hardly any room to lie down. We're spooning an iron girder but it's breaking our back and I'm not sure we can spend the night like this. Shanties, tents, the flash of torches, clanking pots and pans, and our head is thumping, filled with the fumes of a tyre fire. The hand is angry, purple, swollen. We're still alive. Free in a city of shit, whore houses, bridge trolls and boarded up homes. But this is home now, with the bridge trolls and their shanty town. We're shivering and quaking, butting up against the trolls under their newspapers and curling up in stinking sleeping bags. And there's one, now two, maybe three trolls hovering over us; granite statues in dirty drapes, peering at us through stone blue eyes. They pick us up, T., you the fragile body and me the twisted mind, and they dress our hand, find clothes for us in their tents: socks, shoes and a beanie to keep us warm. They sit with us by the fire and share their cooked fish heads, tell us about the bins behind the restaurants in the city centre full of food. They give us a cup to beg with and tell us we can stay as long as we like without questions, interrogation. And now we should sleep, T. Just for a while. Get our strength back.

Panhandle with the trolls tomorrow.

***

A mother and a small girl with an ice cream appear at the foot of the bridge. As they pass, the girl just waggles her finger, mouth open, farting gibberish. She sees us, but she can't tell what she's looking at. We are foreign to her understanding of self; something other.

A filthy alien creature

Or

And the mother is afraid. She shuffles her feet, looks both ways before she crosses the road, ushering her child to the opposite side of the bridge, away from the ugliness, the savagery of poverty and sickness. The smell of unwashed skin and clothes, the acrid piss in the pants, the filth of the arse crack. The dirt on the face, the halitosis and broken teeth. The shit under the long, cracked nails. The jibber jabber from an unclean mind. Because the mother sees the possibility of perversion, moral decline. Compassion is a transaction, an acknowledgement that we exist. It's a point of contact that she's not willing to risk, not willing to teach her daughter. We might infect her, molest her, damage her innocence. We might fuck her up for good.

***

Remember when our mother took us to the zoo, T.? Lions, tigers, chimpanzees. The giraffe, the zebra. Exotic alien creatures brought to earth to entertain us. And we were terrified of the lions at first. They were spent old creatures, their sharp shoulder blades on a pendulum, up and down, in slow motion. A deep sadness in their eyes. They used to rear up to the cage and projectile piss on the people watching, bystanders taking photos. They were documenting their freedom of spirit, their wilful non-compliance to the civilised world, locked in a cage without food or water to slowly die. There were pigs they whipped to perform tricks for a gleeful audience. By the food trucks, there was an orangutang in a tiny cage, an orange shag carpet packed away, folding out of the holes, its chest rising and falling at a whisper, its mouth desperate for air or water or food, its eyes, far away, deep in orangutang space. A victim of the holocaust. Click… click… take a picture for the folks back home. Mother let us get a photo with the tiger cub. They plonked its lifeless body down in our lap, and it sucked the milk from the keeper's baby bottle, tiger heroin. Mother smiled for the first time in a while, still scratching her arms and rushing us off home so she could get her night underway. We wanted to see the snakes before we left but mother wouldn't let us. She said that snakes are slimy bastards, and you can't trust them. Better than a pig though, don't you think, I.? A poor, fat fuck dancing to its master's whip.

***

Other passersby nod and smile. Perfunctory acknowledgments of existence. Some drop a coin or two into the cup without even looking at us. A rolling walrus in a double-breasted suit puts ten dollars in our cup and says, "When will you people learn."

Spit on him, T.! Fucking rip his fat man suspenders! Shove his money up his arsehole! By the end of the day, we have enough for hot chips wrapped up in a newspaper, and we share them with the trolls around the fire. The hand is getting better in the troll dressing. The trolls seem less foreign, foreboding. The burrow next door is heaving, full of meerkats and their punters, the red light seeping out into the river.

***

Mildred's delicate hands, her acidic breath. The smell of the jasmine candle burning on her writing desk. The perfumed water, the feeling of her against us. Millie's haunting theme. And we are living with the trolls. We are truly 'other'. Would she wash our feet now? But maybe she is gone for good, decomposing, sweetening the breath of the river with her drugstore perfume, no gravestone to mark her body at rest. Only our stilted epitaph, fragments of memory and dreams of an arcadian peace in the calm under the agitated surface of the river..

Meerkat absent lover   *deep sea western pearl*

golden figurehead

jasmine tea

nonchalant cigarette   ·   *perched by the window*   *papers*
locked in a drawer

a smile locked in a photo frame   a shoebox full of
money

a forgotten engagement ring   a liquor cabinet

cigar smoke

three dresses

two pairs of shoes

a locked cabinet   occasional gambler

an invisible citizen

a deck of tarot cards

few words of wisdom

constant liar   unflappable

controlled anger

a music box   a
note from the landlord

a knock on the door   another sad man   blowing his
brains out with the whores

a heroine making something beautiful

with her hands

but we never understood we wanted to make things with our mind

our imagination

swinging through vines   with the
monkeys

skipping school
just a baby then
setting fires

building a spaceship from the
sleeping under the stars   trees
and the leaves

discovering new worlds
galaxy queen

finding alien races

or just in the river

bloated
no more hours in the burrow   in absentia   a
funeral for a missing Jane Doe an absent-minded

priest   stumbles over her name

no eulogy   no hymns

finger sandwiches

all done by midday   and we're
the only one

who remembers   who understood her

loved her

we could build her out of blocks of wood
and newspapers

wire and sticky tape   locked in a wire frame

the eyes wouldn't look right

glass replicas

synthetic

eyelashes

we talked about it   after a few whiskeys one night leaving it all behind

the smiles were real on both our faces   arm in arm

spinning circles around the bedroom   ballroom dancer

confidante

Inamorata,

Millie

***

"Whatever you do, don't stop taking the medication suddenly."

Our hands are shaking now, and it's moving up our arms into our neck. A full body fit is coming. The doctor's poison, the fangs of the snakes. We've been here before, T., but this will be a fresh hell this time.

***

A buzzing on the flesh, electric eels, coursing across our skin. Taught, around our calves and ankles, our wrists. We are levitating, under the spell of these electric convulsions. And then the weight, on the legs, pinning down the arms, a fleshy mass rolling over our face, into our eyes, into our mouth, around our neck, tightening, squeezing. Suffocating. It's licking our cheek with its forked tongue, licking our eyeballs. Threatening with every movement to strike, sinks its fangs into our granite flesh. End us with a single impulse. *Don't move, T.*

***

Days of snakes in buildings, bridges, haircuts, shirts, eyeballs, mirrors, ceilings, floors, toilet bowls, sinks, garbage bins, puddles, gutters, drains, trees, windows, letterboxes. The slither in the iris, the twisting of cold scales around our cornea. Reptilian flesh, cold, clammy arms and hands. Gaping wound on the palm, seeping tiny snakes in the blood system, poisoning the whole. The presto of a wild orchestra emanating from the sky! And the fucking fat walrus with his ten-dollar bill, do him like the butcher! We follow him home with a can of gasoline and a book of matches. Tie him up. Douse him in petrol, shove petrolsoaked rags in his mouth and light the match. He burns from the inside out and his squeals are stifled by the fire in his throat. And when he's done, we stick an apple in his mouth, so his wife knows he's cooked. And we don't forget the kindness of these trolls. We might even bring the walrus back cooked to the bridge fire, so we can share his succulent walrus meat and go to sleep fat and happy. Now we're reeling down main street, on to the hardware store to buy supplies for the walrus hunt, and the snakes are filling up the sky and blotting out the sun. They're tearing through the universe, eating the stars with their tiny fangs and we can't see the present let alone the future. Our brain is on fire with flaming snakes, and we need them out of us, out of our eyes, out of this reality, out of all understanding of time and space! But look, now we are a snake, T. Slithering our way across the main street pavement, under the bus, through the business district up to the top of the town hall! Swinging at the top of the flagpole looking down on the city below.

"We will poison every living being in this city, gouging your flesh with our fangs! We are a Reptilian God!"

Were we talking out loud? We must have been.

Three blue boys sitting on us, twisting our arms behind our back, digging their fingers into the bloody palm of our hand. And the sedative is fast, as we're tied down in the back of the ambulance full of snakes and trolls and walruses. A menagerie of exotic mind animals bouncing down the sea of snakes, out to the reptilian highway.

***

Z Ward

A dream I think, T. Three arched glass windows, outside

an alien wasteland, a colony

Shuffling feet

Rotten

underwear and jumpsuits

Garbled voices

The banging of batons on wood   Crossed arms,

smug laughter

Garbage, sweat, piss and shit, the headiness of bleach does

little to disguise it all.[1]

---

[1] Amidst the smells, mingling together, the smell of neglected
humanity, there is only hopelessness. It is a smell so rotten, so old,
it is just dust catching in the nostrils. There is an absence of
dreams, of freedom. They are relegated to the nights, locked in
cells, slowly drifting further into the darkness of forgetfulness.

Pushed out into a vibrant yard of native trees and green

lawn.   Warble, T. Get their attention[2]

                    Psychotic darting eyes of birds, beaks

        squawking melodious gibberish

    Wind undulating quietly

Scavenger birds[3]

    Groaning

    Digging

---

[2] A harsh slope meets the foot of the wall, too hard to climb, tall
enough that the sun is just winking over the top of it.

[3] One of the birds stays with us, in our gravitational pull. It is a
moment of trust or perhaps curiosity. A loud squawk and the bird
takes flight, baring off into the skyline, past the tree and behind Z
Ward.

"You using that stick?"[4]

A stick cracking, hard on our back[5]

"Welcome to Z Ward."

Only the sound of the *wind*…

They're on him. They're beating him like a wire puppet, T.! He's on fire![6]

---

[4] A low gruff voice, a thick, blistered hand outstretched. A collection of meat stuffed inside a set of overalls, a big, bald head with the remaining hair falling down his ears and in a mullet at the back. He's got those crazy eyes, and a big angry beak, his forehead all clenched up in the anticipation of violence. So, should we give him the stick? Just do what he says.

[5] And the blows rain down on us, the whipping pain through our legs and flank. He catches us in the temple, and we fall down like a disconnected set of appendages, buckling under our own weight.
[6] As the blue-sky mottles in our eyes, our hand floating in space somewhere between our face and the sun, the bully boys are on him, beating him with the big clubs, taking him down. His overalls are all rolled up and his legs are wire cages stuffed full of old newspapers, a poupée, just like the one they put in windows to scare off the robbers. And he's convulsing, this wire puppet, as they pin him down and beat him on the legs and on his back.

The blanket puts out the fire[7]

Grunting

        Screaming and thrashing

                silence

        Birds in the trees, squawking, screaming[8]

             The scavenger

birds pinned to the wall in the ditch

    The smell of burning flesh

---

[7] The bully boys put a blanket on the burning puppet man, the flames splutter out, and we can rest our head on the ground and close our eyes.

[8] The old gum tree full of confused birds, squawking and screeching, complaining about all the fuss, wary of the flightless, scavenger birds cowering by the wall, in the ditch.

The door locks behind us[9]

Sleep

Shuffling   Grunting

                    moaning

Baton's banging on the doors

The sour smell of bodies

Mottled sun through the caged window

---

[9] The cold, darkness of the bird coop. The hope is gone, and we are tired enough to sleep, even if it is fitfully, our head still aching from the blows of the stick.

The chatter of men's voices[10]

The birds spook, fizzing

out of the tree into the blue sky

The sounds of hooves

beating along the line of the wall

Whinnies and grunts

The smell of hay and manure

A flurry of anxious voices

---

[10] We can see, out our cell window, five great Clydesdales pulling a
wagon topped with men, bags and packages. Where are we, T.?
Over a hundred years in the wrong direction.

The crack of a gunshot!

Demands barked by the most exotic bird[11]

Just the wind again

A dream, T. Lost in dreams

The birds return to their chatter

A woman is crying

----

[11] There is the most splendid sight. An exotic bird, beautiful plumage, so much colour, so much more unique than the scavenger birds in Z Ward. It is a boy, no, a tiny man with a thick beard, riding resplendent on the back of an ostrich, shimmering gold jewellery around his neck, long, sleek pistols in either hand. The most magnificent bushranger conjured up by the psychosis of the boggy, southern plains. The men on the wagon are terrified, jumping down with their hands raised.

The Ship of Fools

It must have been days, not weeks. We would never survive weeks in Z Ward. An abrupt whistle, the stomping of feet from outside the cell as the door swings open heavily. The exotic birds in their cages squawk in panic as we are dragged out by our ears, beaten with clubs, rushed down the stairs and shoved into the back of the waiting cart. One moment of freedom, the sounds and smells of the marshland air, the distorted limbs of trees hanging melancholically over the dirt road, a glissando of deciduous notes floating downward, resting gently on the earth. Bystanders watch on in interest. Even children pause their imaginary games to gawk at us. The drudgery of the cart through bushland and small towns, a parade of the criminally insane, unwashed and clawing onto the bars of the cab windows, these wide-eyed scavenger birds, captives of the state, contained madness made public spectacle. And the rocks ding off the sides of the cab as the children run behind, spooking the prisoners, the cart rocking down the dirt road. The Clydesdales' hooves beat out a steady rhythm, a death march. Their shit fills our nostrils, that acrid smell of a well-fed horse that burns the back of the throat. The sun is setting by the time we can smell the sea and the filth of the port. Salt and oil. Rotten fish heads and the barking of angry dogs. We can see, through the barred window, the sun sitting on top of the horizon, bleeding orange and purple, and the smoke haze rising from the port, a black eye on the face of the dimly lit sky. The crash of waves, the rankness of the rotten clams, the mechanical pullies of cranes, winches, automated pneumatic arms releasing gas, picking up bodies from the harbour and releasing them into mass graves, picked at by the manic gulls, fighting amongst themselves for scraps of skin, meat, eyeballs. We feel the horses slow to a halt by the entry to the canal. Perhaps this is how it ends, T. The place where we might find Mildred amongst the discarded food scraps and Christmas ornaments, in the bottom of the pit, amongst the rotting bodies, clawed by blackened fingernails. Her exposed blue breasts, the flesh of her backside, her broken neck and awkwardly turned head, mouth agape, dry lolling tongue, skewed eyes fixed in opposite directions. We will be another naked member of the dumpsite soon enough. Our madness all for nothing, our lifeforce a scattered memory, an off-colour joke in a pub somewhere, the old, confused drunkard's thoughts bubbling up out of his beer.

The cab doors explode, orange light pouring over us. And they drag us out, pulling us backward, picking us up, gripping our arms, making us walk our last few steps, shoving their meat fists into our back. The wind is fierce in opposition, a wall of roaring sound. But it is not the pit that we are being taken to. Something more macabre, more splendid is in store for us. In front of us, a beautiful, wooden ship creaks and sways, its mast stabbing deep into the cortex of a darkening sky. There is the smell of cadaverous fish, meat hanging on the delicate bones, salt and seaweed. And the port is a mill of confused agitation. Bodies in rags are dragged to the ladder, forced on board. A priest in white robes on the deck, directs them down to the galley. He is a splendiferous goose with a white coat and bright yellow beak. He burns bright in the growing darkness, his stiff biretta, an exclamation point, above his head. They prod us up the ladder and we make our way down below. The darkness is complete now, just the rumbling of stomachs, the moaning of despair, the maniacal laughter of confusion and resignation. Below it all, the orchestra pulses, a rising and falling series of staccato strings, the legato woodwinds and brass glowing between them, a triumphant cacophony of chaos and confusion. And we wait, amongst the piss and the shit, the farting rabble. We can feel the rough hands groping our legs, exploring our face, dirty fingers in our mouth, our nose. Cries from the deck and the ship is moving, T.! It is rolling and pitching, soon the sails catch the fierce wind, and we can feel it. We are gone, deep in the darkness, the night above us now, the white goose priest steering us toward our salvation.

Hours of atrophying muscles and mind-numbing constraint, light seeps through the cracks in the wood above us, and by morning the bolts are unlatched. A mutinous sea of bodies pours out the hatch to take in our new reality: endless blue, the ripple of the surface of the ocean, infinite. The sail slaps slackly against the mast. We are at the whim of the sea. The goose priest speaks loudly from the bow. We are to find a new home across the ocean, outcasts, wayfarers, the unclean minds detached from the body of our homeland.
The motley crew of beggars and madmen begin to stir. Eruptions of angry shouts and grumbles, the clenching of fists, the tension in the crude necks of the accidental sailors.

"There is rum and salted meat in the galley where you slept. It could be a long journey. Self-discipline will be the key." But it is clear the goose priest is half-drunk himself, swaying and slurring his words, muck on the bottom of his cassock, his biretta pointing north-east.

A flock of angry seagulls, elbows and fingers, beaks biting at flesh, flew back down the hatch, rummaging amongst the crates and the supplies, and we sway on the deck, the burn of the rum in our throat as we wash down great swigs, gulping and burping and laughing for the first time in a long time. There is a sing-song Filipino sailor, with his merry tunes and cheers, clinking bottles. The encroaching storm on the horizon seems so far away. There is the vomit over the side, the groping and pinching of the younger boys by the bullies handing out the rum. As the rain begins to spit on the deck, greasing up our hair, the fights inevitably break out. The uncontrolled violence, bottled up, is released by the soaking of the rum in the unbalanced brains. And when the fighting stops, the bodies all tired out on the deck, bloodied and bruised, heavy drops of cold rain begin to scatter across them and we grow colder and colder, shivering. The rum has taken its effect on us too, T. The horizon tilts up and down, a broken gyroscope. Sudden vomit, sicking up on our ragged shirt. The clouds surround us, pitch black, the eye of the sky closing up, the storm punching its way across the face of the universe. Suddenly, the boat rocks violently, bodies clinging to the mast, losing grip and flying into the unforgiving ocean. Look up, T. There he is, the goose priest, whipped by the wind and the rain, standing tall on the bird's nest at the top of the mast, his hands outstretched putting his fate in the hands of the storm. A sudden explosion of lightning shooting him from the mast and flinging him across the sea, his screams barely heard behind the din of the storm. Miles away, his body disappears into the angry blackness of the raging ocean. And we pray, T. There is nothing else for it. We put our face in our hands, and we pray to God that this will all end, that we will wake up and find ourselves in Mildred's arms as she slowly runs her fingers through our hair. We can hear the angelic choirs of heaven breaking through the storm clouds as we picture Mother, cradling us as an infant, humming her songs gently to us. And we see her at her last moment, crumpled in the bed, emaciated, a wretched life ending with a whimper, the pianissimo last tones of the clarinets sounding the final notes of her restless symphony.

Boom! We are sent skittering across the deck, rum soaked bodies flying over the bow. A rock, a great shark biting through the hull, wood splintering and exploding, and the ship is no longer a ship, now just a collection of parts. A great wave throws us high overboard, smacking us hard into the water. We are deep down, writhing and fighting for our life. Above us, at the surface, is a dark bowl of destruction, floating bodies, jagged splinters of wood, a seething, elemental sky pouring its fury down upon us. All of this, but below the surface it is quiet. Just the far-off booms of thunder, the garbled screams and shouts of desperate men. We shoot to the surface, flailing our arms, our lungs filling with water. Another huge wave picks us up, smashing us back down to the ocean floor. It is too much, T. Mildred's fingers clench our throat, squeezing the last gasp of air from our lungs. The shame washes over us, the distant, lost shame of a life lived without reason or purpose. We close our eyes and submit, letting our lifeless body be violently moved at the whim of the raging ocean. And at this final moment of despair, as the dissonance of the music moves to its final resolution, suddenly, the waters part. Two great hands reach down and pluck us from the ocean, pulling us from our wretched fate. Our mother's hands, T., pulling us from the bath water.

We loll and gasp and splutter, a helpless child held tightly against her shoulder. She wraps a towel around us, patting us on the back to spit up the water.

We can hear her heartbeat fast through her chest and her whispering to us, "Shh… Shh…". We are safe here in our mother's arms, T. But we cannot stay here for long. This broken mind will not allow it.

***

Angelic Robot Voices

Cosmic spin cycle. The bolts rusted, hinges creaking. Violent, epileptic shudders… The carcass of the washing machine advances over the ravined plains of our brain. It spews out grey water, half washed clothes and dead animals found under trees and behind the sink. A sickening blackness is in the door, the eye of it, whirling, stop-start, screaming metal frame with the final death throes of an aged, mechanical beast. And it rumbles through the wrinkles of our cerebral cortex, in search of an idea that will give its dying moments purpose. We must wait for it to die, T. There's nothing we can do to kill it. On the outside, all we've got is darkness, a weight on our eyes, like a cloth or sack. And we can't move, not a finger. Everything's pinned down in heavy straps, even the forehead pinned to a hard metal slab. Ammonia, the smell of it, its thick presence gets through the weight over our face, jammed in our nostrils, a dense tongue dipped in bleach. We are cold, T., but our body doesn't have the strength, the capacity, to shiver. We are trembling inside with the unrecognised potential of movement.

Now listen. A humming church choir singing a single note, perpetually playing loudly enough to occupy us entirely. It slowly twists and bends, the shepherd's tone. We need to break this sensory saturation of monotony. How long will this go on? No, it is our turn. Take the stagnant, humming note and embellish it. Add new harmonies in the mind born of a rudimentary understanding of western composition. The harmony makes beautiful, ethereal music. The counterpoint constructed in the imagination; polyphonic, spontaneous, and improvised. The harmonies building organically through a sea of voices. Angelic robot voices lifting us from the cold, metal slab, up and out into the assumption of darkness. And now we shiver, vibrate! We glow a million shades of bursting light. And maybe we have made it, T. Maybe this is heaven!...

Until it falters, the music drifting away in disjointed phrases; a cacophony of half remembered melodies, clashing bells, the dissonance of the harmonic series.

The light is snuffed, a wisp of ethereal smoke looking for a way out of the black. We are smothered, restrained. We are helpless. The returning hum of the perpetual note, that smell of ammonia. We must be alive then, if we can hear and we can smell, if we can see enough to know that there is nothing there. Should we dream? Dream of old, discarded washing machines, ripped, bald tyres, smashed computer screens, rats living in bags of garbage? Maybe dream of angelic choirs, cosmic collisions, the holy release of breaching the limits of mortality.

That hum again, T. That one note symphony, bubbles up in the brain, like they've been waiting in here the whole time. A shuffle of feet. A man's voice? No, not human. And someone disturbing something metal. The needle's quick fire in the arm and you are gone, T. Numb. You can still hear me, taste the air, the ammonia. Sudden light, and a hand over our face. A robotic hand with metal fingers and an eye of light on the top of its head. The metal fingers are whirring, moving across the top of our head, but we can't feel anything. I can hear it, the buzz of electricity. *Buzz.* An electric trephination. Lubricated pads attached to the skull, electrical fingertips, wayward currents coursing around the flaps of brain tissue, fishing. They're looking for me, T. They're trying to cut out the infection. Cleanse the mind. But I'm hiding behind the amygdala. They're moving into the frontal lobe. Wrapping around the brain stem. They won't find me. They can't. They're shining lights in our eyes and aiming the current on the left hemisphere, making us talk - *Cunt! Fucker! Areola!* The words just come blurting out like therapy. And it could be hours, days even. These techno aliens sure don't muck around. And when they leave the room, we can start to feel our skin vibrating. We can move our head enough to see the window, flooded with darkness, punctured with the light of a million stars. Deep space. I knew it, T. We're way out now. When the robotic alien comes back in, he shoots us with another needle and we're deep in the well.

***

I lug your bony arse down imaginary hallways

Up imaginary flights of stairs

Over the ledge of an imaginary rooftop But

we never hit the ground in a dream Not

in a dream at least.

***

And those robots sent us back, T., right back to the facility. You back in your wheelchair by the window. The bully boys, the doctors, the rats scurrying around with the connect four and someone brought in some tarot cards which set off half the wing in flights of imagination. They locked the revolving door, so they won't lose us again. You know, you could go forty-nine years with only one visitor in a place like this, and it would probably just be a lawyer wondering why you hadn't been lodging your taxes. The electrical tests didn't seem to have the slightest effect on us. Although, it's hard to put a lot of things together, you know, like they happened. Anyway, they never did find me in all that brain fat of yours. The doctors here keep giving us the drugs and the updates on diagnosis, but nothing changes for us. I'm still here and you're still there and never the two shall meet. Those doctors don't believe us, still. They nod and smile, but I'm sure their case notes tell a different story. I think we're way better off this way, anyway, not knowing I mean, whether it's us or them that are wrong in the head. It doesn't matter really. Everyone's story is their own. They choose to believe something, and we choose to believe nothing at all. Can you hear that? Those strings again, those woodwinds. I think that music will be with us forever. A blessing and a curse. Take a sip of your juice there, T., and have a look out the window. Those dandelions are stubborn bastards. Bully boys have been stomping their boots all over them for generations, flicking their cigarette ash on their petals. But no matter what they throw at them, those dandelions just keep coming back more beautiful than ever.

***

Fin.

GREIG THOMSON is an author living and working in Adelaide, South Australia. After hanging out at the University of Adelaide for a year or two, he completed his Bachelor of Arts and received a First Class Honours in Creative Writing. A swift change of direction led him into the world of publishing, establishing his publishing house, *Disarticulated Press* in the following year. His work can be found in literary journals across the world, including *Orca Literary Journal*, *Watershed Review*, *God's Cruel Joke Literary Magazine*, *Ginosko Literary Journal*, and many more.

DISARTICULATED PRESS bubbled around in the brain of its founder, Greig Thomson, in the year after his time at the University of Adelaide. Meeting likeminded authors, equally disillusioned by the state of the publishing industry, Thomson decided to create his own literary press, to better serve the non-compliant, subversive, and widely ignored by the mainstream publishing brands. *Disarticulated Press* encourages voices with an edge, shouting to the skies or whispering into the darkness. All are welcome. To find out more, visit, *disarticulatedpress.com*

ISBN 978-1-7642019-0-2